The Brave Warrior's Lesson

A North American Tale

Retold by Sally Cowan
Illustrations by Joseph Qiu

Contents

Chapter 1

The Warrior Comes Back

There was once a brave warrior.
He had been away from his people
for many years
and had just come back to his village.

The people wanted to know
what he had been doing for all that time.
So, he told them about the people he had met,
and the animals he had hunted.

Each story was more exciting than the last.
But, after a while,
the warrior began to boast.

"No warrior is braver than me!" he shouted,
"and no hunter is stronger!
There is no one in the world
who would dare to disobey me!"

A young woman stepped out of her wigwam.

"I know someone who will not obey you," she said. "He does whatever he wants."

The warrior looked at her in surprise.

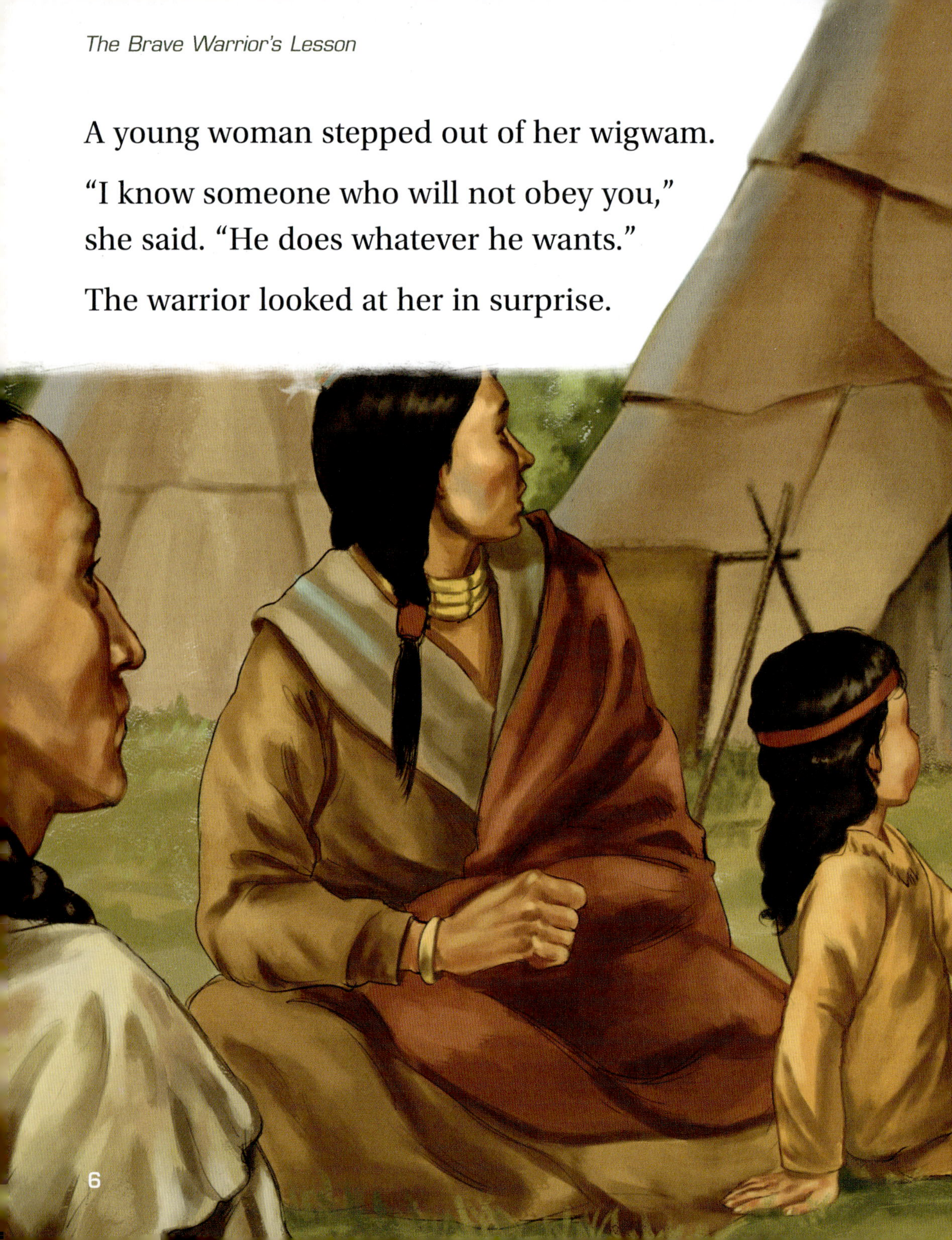

"Well," he said. "Who is he?
He must be as tall as a giant!"

"No," said the woman. "He is not very tall."

"Is he stronger than a buffalo?" he asked.

“Oh, no,” she laughed. “He is not very strong.”

“Then he must know magic!” said the warrior.

“No,” said the woman. “He doesn’t know any magic.”

"Well, take me to him!" he said.
"Then we will see if he is so brave
as to disobey me."

The woman turned towards her wigwam.
"Come on," she said. "Please follow me."

"What?" said the warrior.
"Does he live in this village?"

The woman nodded,
and showed the warrior into her home.

Chapter 2

The Baby

The warrior looked around the wigwam,
but he could only see a small baby,
sitting on a rug.
The baby was happily playing with a little toy.

"Well, where is he?" asked the warrior,
who was getting quite annoyed.

The woman pointed to her baby.
"There he is," she said.

The warrior laughed.
"Ah, this is a joke!" he said.

"No, not at all," the woman said.
"I think that my baby will not obey you."

Now, the woman knew that the warrior
had never had to look after a baby,
and that he did not know what babies were like.

The warrior rolled his eyes.

"Very well, then," he said, "this will be easy!"

He knelt down on one knee
and smiled at the baby.

"Come here, little one!" he said gently.
"Come to me!"

But the baby didn't look up,
and went on playing with his toy.

The warrior had another idea.
He began to whistle some beautiful bird calls.

“Oh, what lovely bird calls!” said the woman.
“But my baby hardly seems to notice them.”

She was right.
The baby went on playing with his toy.

The warrior looked at the woman in surprise. "Why won't your baby come to me? Can't he hear me?" he asked.

The woman just smiled.

"Come here, baby!" he said, in a louder voice.

But when the warrior leaned forward and spoke, the baby dropped the toy and started to cry.

Chapter 3

A Lesson

The warrior had one last idea.
He began to sing in a soft, kindly voice.

The baby stopped crying,
gave a big yawn and closed his eyes.
The song had made him sleepy!

The warrior felt very foolish.
He knew now that he should not have boasted.
He quietly stood up
and walked out of the wigwam.

The woman picked up her sleepy baby.

"The warrior has learned a lesson today,"
she whispered, as she placed the baby in his little bed.
"Even brave warriors can't have everything their own way."